Party Train

By Lesli Mitchell

Dedicated to my son, Connor,
who taught me about love and courage through his example.

Illustrations by Ramon Gil

Text Copyright © 2001 Lesli Mitchell
Illustration Copyright © 2001 Ramon Gil

Published by:

DRL Books, Inc.
12 West 18th Street
New York, NY 10011
Phone: 800 853 1057
212 604 9637
Fax: 212 206 9329

Email: julie@difflearn.com

ISBN: 0-9668266-1-9
Library of Congress Card Number 2001094243

Printed in Hong Kong

Here's a shiny new steam engine. But he's all alone.
Do you want to add a car to the steam engine?

Say, "Yes!"

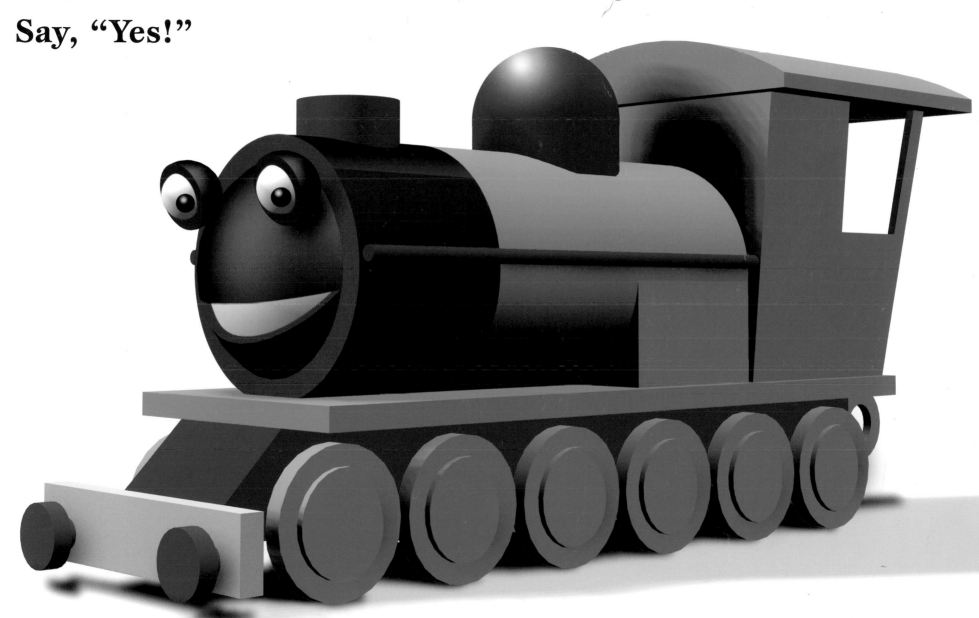

You did it! Now we have a blue car in our train.

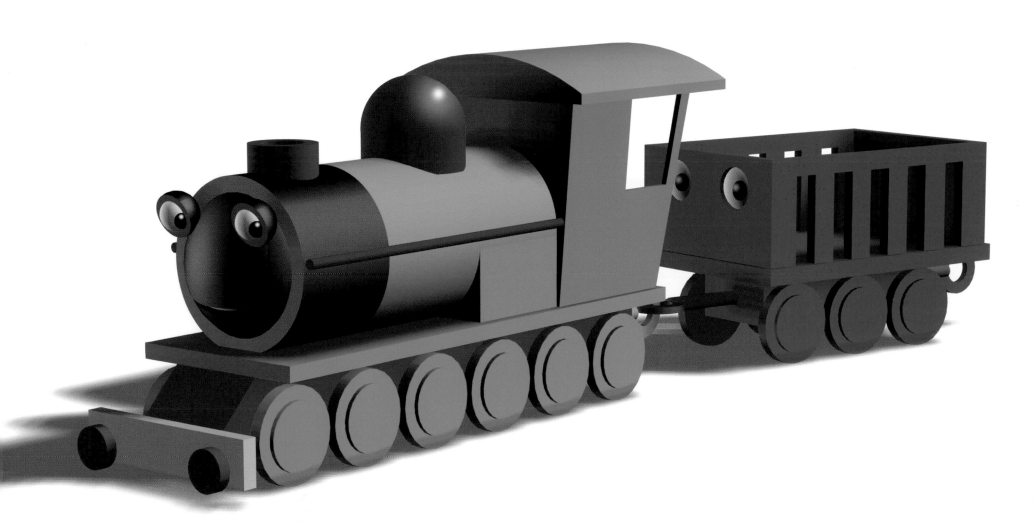

But wait — it's empty!
Let's put a giraffe in the blue car.
Say, "Want giraffe!"

6

Great! There's our giraffe.
And look, he's smiling at you.
Say, "Hi, giraffe!"

Good saying hi to the giraffe.

What's the giraffe doing now?
He's looking at the back of the train.
I think he wants a friend.

This time, let's add a car and an animal to our train.
You ready? **Say, "Want car and animal!"**

Good talking! Now we've got a yellow car and a red dinosaur.

Something's not right, though. The dinosaur is just standing there beside the train.

Look! Now he's pointing to the yellow car.
I think he wants to go inside.

Do you think we should
put him in the car?

Say, "Put dinosaur in car."

Oh, no! We messed up!
They're stuck in the same car!
**Say, "Put dinosaur
in yellow car."**

You did it! Whew — that was a close one. Thank you for helping. The animals like to have their very own cars.

Hey, know what? We could add some more cars and make our train even bigger.
Say, "I want more cars!" Can you say "please," too?

That was a very nice please,
and it worked! You've got
two more cars.
What color are they?

Say, "Orange and green."

You're right. The cars look sad, though. I think they want some animal friends. We want a happy train, so we better get some friends — fast!

Say, "We need friends, fast!"

Good talking! Now we've got two new animals in their very own cars. Who are your new animal friends?

Say, "Whale and butterfly."

That's right.
And everybody is smiling.
Do we have a happy train now?

Say, "Yes, happy train!"

Hey, do you see something different? The whale has a hat on.
And not just any hat — it looks like a party hat!
Do you want to have a party for the train?

Say, "Yes, I want party!"

You did it! You've got a party train now!
Look at all of those party hats.

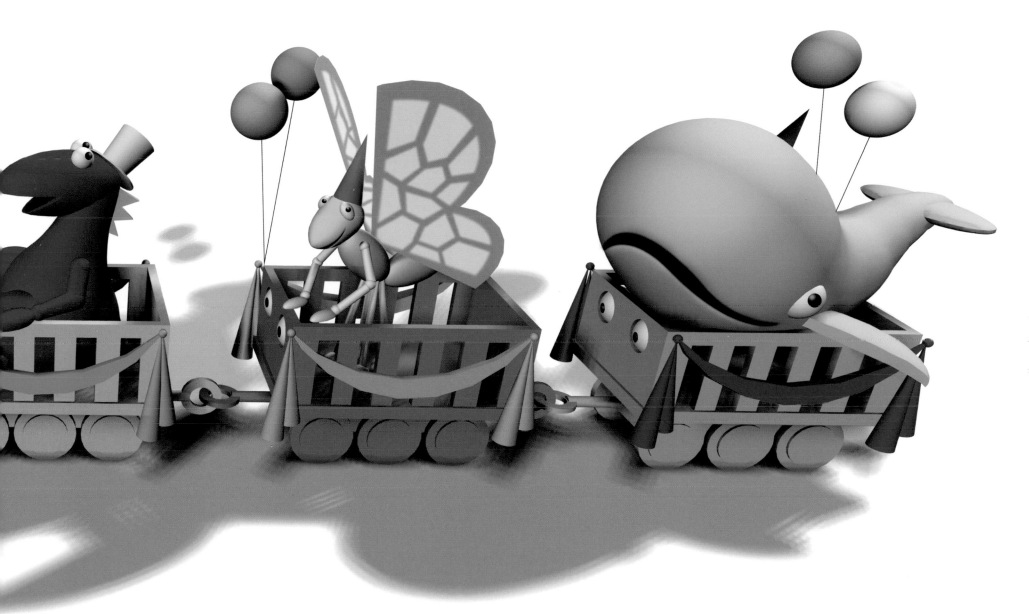

Do you see the balloons and the ribbons, too? **Say, "Yes!"**

The animals are looking around — maybe we forgot something. Hmm, what else do you have at a party?

It's not really a party without cake and ice cream. Let's get your friends some food to eat.

Say, "Need cake and ice cream!"

Good job! I think the animals like your cake and ice cream.

Look at the whale — he's eating two pieces of cake!

What's the butterfly doing? I think she's sharing some cake with the whale. Very nice! Whales eat a lot of cake, you know.

Do you think they're thirsty now? Maybe we could give the animals some juice, too.

Say, "Give juice to animals."

Good job!
I think the steam engine
was very thirsty!

The animals like your party train.
Do you like your party train, too?

Say, "Yes, I like my party train!"

Now your friends are ready to go for a ride.
But the train is just sitting there — it's not moving one bit!

What do we need to make the train go?
Say, "We need tracks!"

You did it! The animals are very excited.
They love your new tracks!

They're ready to go for a ride.

Hey! The train is still not moving!
Your friends are looking at you.

I think they want you
to tell the train to go.

Let's try again.

Say, "Go forward, train!"

Yay! The train is going forward! Good job telling the train to go.

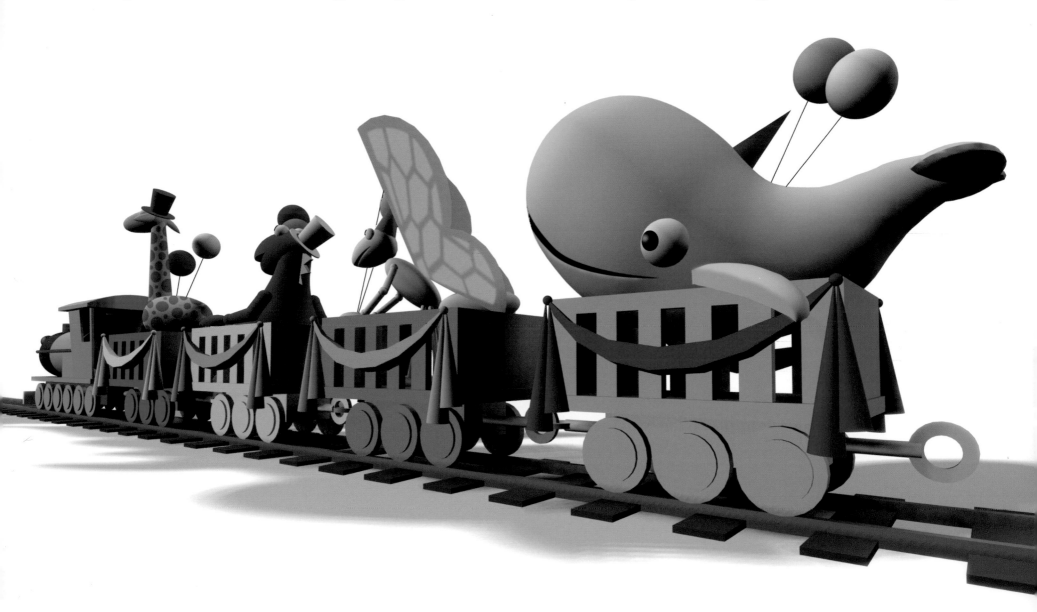

Oh, no! The train kept going! Look — it's going off the page!
Do you want the train to come back?

Say, "Come back, train!"

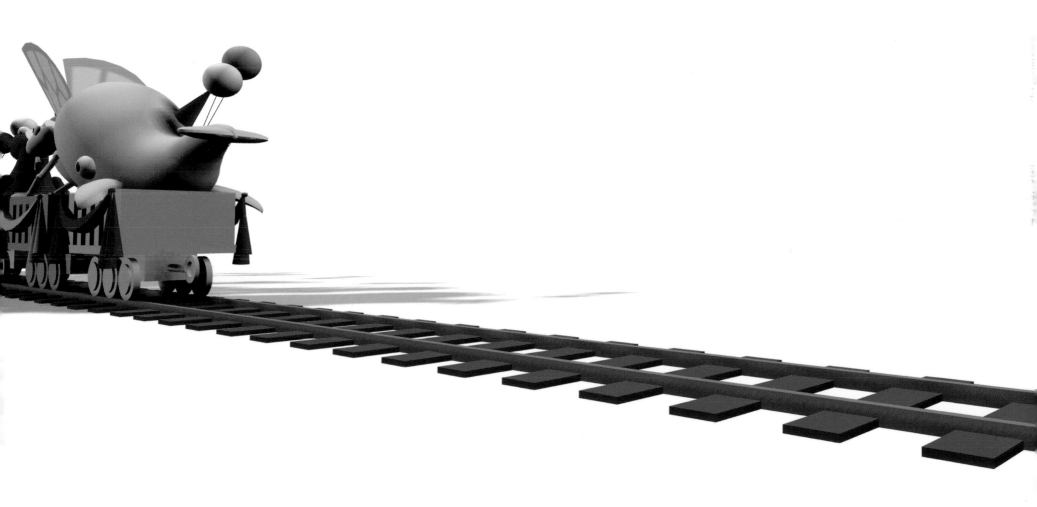

You did it! Our party train is back! All of your animal friends are waving to you.

Say, "Hi animals!"

Good saying hi to the animals.

What are they doing now? They're dancing on your party train! And they look very happy.
Are you happy, too?

Say, "Yes, I'm happy!"

They're happy you're happy.
They like playing with you.
Thank you for a great party!

Hey, do you see one of the animals yawning? Who's getting tired? **Say, "Butterfly is tired."**

Look! Now the other animals are yawning, too.
And the cars. And the steam engine.
Do you think the party train
needs a nap?

Say, "Time to nap, party train."
Oops, we better whisper.
Say quietly, "Time to nap, party train."

It worked. The train is sleeping now. You did a great job making a party train. **Say, "I did it! Yay!"**

Now say it louder. "I DID IT!! YAY!!" (It's OK — you won't wake up the train.) What do you want to do while the train is sleeping? **Use your words and say, "I want to..."**